Note to parents, carers and teachers

Read it yourself is a series of modern stories, favourite characters and traditional tales written in a simple way for children who are learning to read. The books can be read independently or as part of a guided reading session.

Each book is carefully structured to include many high-frequency words vital for first reading. The sentences on each page are supported closely by pictures to help with understanding, and to offer lively details to talk about.

The books are graded into four levels that progressively introduce wider vocabulary and longer stories as a reader's ability and confidence grows.

Ideas for use

- Although your child will now be progressing towards silent, independent reading, let her know that your help and encouragement is always available.

- Developing readers can be concentrating so hard on the words that they sometimes don't fully grasp the meaning of what they're reading. Answering the puzzle questions on pages 46 and 47 will help with understanding.

For more information and advice on Read it yourself and book banding, visit **www.ladybird.com/readityourself**

Book Band 10

Level 4 is ideal for children who are ready to read longer stories with a wider vocabulary and are eager to start reading independently.

Special features:

Detailed illustrations to capture the imagination

Clear type

Longer sentences

At Moshi Fun Park, more naughty Moshlings were again shouting at each other and throwing food.

Suddenly, Luvli saw Dr Strangeglove. He was putting out sweets for the Moshlings to find.

"I was right!" said Luvli.

18

Full, exciting story

Richer, more varied vocabulary

Dewy was not in the Games Starcade, but Raarghly was.

"Have you seen Dewy today?" Luvli asked him.

"No," said Raarghly. "Right now, all I want to do is eat. I need food!"

"I'll get you some food as soon as I find Dewy," Luvli said.

GAMES STARCADE

32

33

Educational Consultant: Geraldine Taylor
Book Banding Consultant: Kate Ruttle

A catalogue record for this book is available from the British Library

This edition published by Ladybird Books Ltd 2013
80 Strand, London, WC2R ORL
A Penguin Company

001

The moral right of the author and illustrator has been asserted.

Ladybird, Read It Yourself and the Ladybird Logo are registered or
unregistered trademarks of Ladybird Books Limited.

ISBN: 978-0-72327-529-9

Printed in China

Luvli
and the
Glump-a-tron

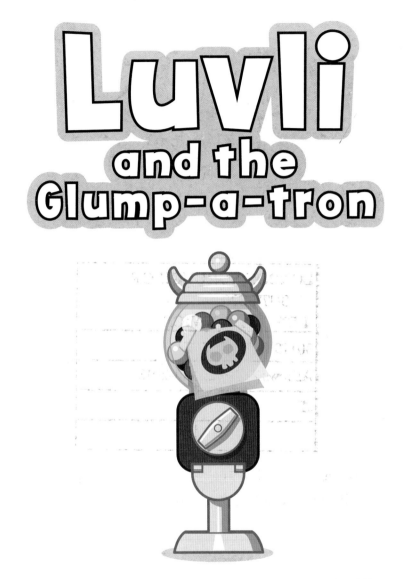

Written by Ronne Randall
Illustrated by Fran and David Brylewska

One day, Luvli came to see Buster Bumblechops and the Moshlings at Buster's ranch.

The Moshlings there were eating sweets, shouting at each other and throwing food around.

Luvli looked all around the ranch for Buster Bumblechops and found him hiding from the Moshlings. There was food all over him!

"Luvli," he said, "I need help!"

Luvli and Buster Bumblechops
hid by the Gumball Machine.

"Why are the Moshlings so
naughty today?" Luvli asked.

"I don't know," said Buster.

Buster looked around the Gumball Machine.

"Look!" he said. "There's something from Dr Strangeglove! He says that he made the Moshlings naughty!"

"How?" asked Luvli.

13

Buster said, "Do you think Dr Strangeglove put something in those sweets to make the Moshlings naughty?"

"Yes," said Luvli. "So I'm going to Monstro City to find out why!"

When Luvli got to Monstro City,
she found more naughty Moshlings.

"So Dr Strangeglove got to these
Moshlings, too!" she thought.
"I'm going to Moshi Fun Park.
Maybe he'll be there."

At Moshi Fun Park, more naughty Moshlings were again shouting at each other and throwing food.

Suddenly, Luvli saw Dr Strangeglove. He was putting out sweets for the Moshlings to find.

"I was right!" said Luvli.

19

Luvli went over to Dr Strangeglove at once. "Stop putting out those sweets right now!" she said. "All the Moshlings who eat them are turning naughty!"

"These sweets are doing just what I want them to," said Dr Strangeglove. "Now get out my way – I'm going to the Port!"

He laughed and ran off. "Mwah ha ha!"

Luvli ran after Dr Strangeglove, all the way to the Port. But as soon as she got there, a Glump came right at her. Where had it come from?

Suddenly, Luvli saw a machine that was pulling in Moshlings and turning them into Glumps!

"Stop that machine!" Luvli shouted to Dr Strangeglove.

"No!" said Dr Strangeglove. "It's MY Glump-a-tron! Mwah ha ha!"

He made the machine go faster, and it pulled in more and more Moshlings. "Mwah ha ha!" he laughed again.

Just then, some Super Moshis came to help Luvli.

When he saw the Super Moshis, Dr Strangeglove ran off. The Super Moshis ran after him.

Now Luvli just had to work out how to stop the machine.

"I know! Dewy can help me," she thought.

Luvli went to Dewy's shop,
but no one was there.

"If Dewy's not in his shop,"
she thought, "he'll be in the
Games Starcade."

Dewy was not in the Games Starcade, but Raarghly was.

"Have you seen Dewy today?" Luvli asked him.

"No," said Raarghly. "Right now, all I want to do is eat. I need food!"

"I'll get you some food as soon as I find Dewy," Luvli said.

But Poppet could not find Furi.

"I'll just have to stop the Clump-o-tron myself," she thought. "I'll find a way to do it. The Moshlings need my help!"

Lavil looked at the machine. "How can I make it stop?" she thought.

There were some Moshlings holding on to her to keep from being pulled in by the machine. "Help us!" they shouted.

The Moshlings were still holding on to Lavli, and the Glump-o-tron was still pulling them. Now it was pulling Lavli, too!

"Help!" said Lavli. "I have to try and do something – fast!"

Suddenly there was a big THUMP, a big BUMP and the Clump-o-tron stopped.

"What's stopping it?" yelled LAVA. She looked at the machine. The Clump-o-tron had pulled her handbag in.

"My handbag made it stop!" Lavli said.

"We're all right now," said the Great Moshling. "And the Sew Bot battery will be alright. It will work the soup working."

She looked at the tall man's mouth. "It's good that I had my handbag today!" she said, and they all laughed.

GLUM

How much do you remember about the story of Moshi Monsters: Luvli and the Glump-a-tron? Answer these questions and find out!

- Who does Luvli go to see at the beginning?

- Who is making the Moshlings naughty?

- How is he doing this?

- Where does Luvli find Dr Strangeglove?

- What is the Glump-a-tron doing to the Moshlings?

- How does Luvli stop the Glump-a-tron in the end?

Unjumble these words to make characters from the story, then match them to the correct pictures.

Liluv   Breust Blechumpobs

rD Slogarngevet   Ralygrah

Read it yourself with Ladybird

Tick the books you've read!